P9-DIY-385

To Donna and Martha

Balzer + Bray is an imprint of HarperCollins Publishers.

First Snow
Copyright © 2015 by Peter McCarty
All rights reserved. Manufactured in China.
No part of this book may be used or reproduced in any manner whatsoever without written
permission except in the case of brief quotations embodied in critical articles and reviews.
For information address HarperCollins Children's Books, a division of HarperCollins Publishers,
195 Broadway, New York, NY 10007.
www.harpercollinschildrens.com

ISBN 978-0-06-218996-7

The art for this book was done on Fabriano 140 lb. hot press watercolor paper with Sennelier
shellac-based colored inks and Winsor and Newton watercolors.
Typography by Martha Rago
14 15 16 17 18   SCP   10 9 8 7 6 5 4 3 2 1
❖
First Edition

Peter McCarty

FIRST SNOW

BALZER + BRAY
An Imprint of HarperCollins*Publishers*

From the window, Sancho and his sisters could see that their special visitor had finally arrived. He had traveled from far away all by himself.

"Say hello to your cousin Pedro," said their mother.

"Hello, Pedro!" said Sancho, Bella, Lola, Ava, and Maria.

"It's starting to snow, Pedro," said Sancho.

"I have never seen snow. I don't think I will like it," said Pedro.

"Why not?"

"Because it is cold. And I don't like cold."

"Wake up, Pedro!"

Sancho, Bella, Lola, Ava, and Maria were excited. It had snowed all night long!

"Put on your boots! Put on your coat! Put on your hat and mittens!
We are going outside!"

"It is cold," said Pedro.

"You have to move around to stay warm," said Sancho.

"We are making snow angels!" said Bella, Lola, Ava,

and Maria. "You make one too, Pedro!"

"I don't want to lie down in the snow. It is cold."

Just then the neighborhood children came by. "This is my cousin
Pedro," said Sancho. "He has never seen snow before."

"Hello, Pedro!" they all said.

"Isn't it wonderful how the snowflakes float around," said Abby. "You can even catch them on your tongue. It tastes good!"

"It tastes cold," said Pedro.

"Hey, Pedro, grab a sled," said Henry. "We're
going up to the top of the big hill!"

"Why do you go up?" asked Pedro.

"To go back down," said Henry.

From the top of the hill, the children could see the
whole world below.

"You go first, Pedro," said Henry.

"Oh no, not me!"

"Bridget and I will go first!" said Chloe.

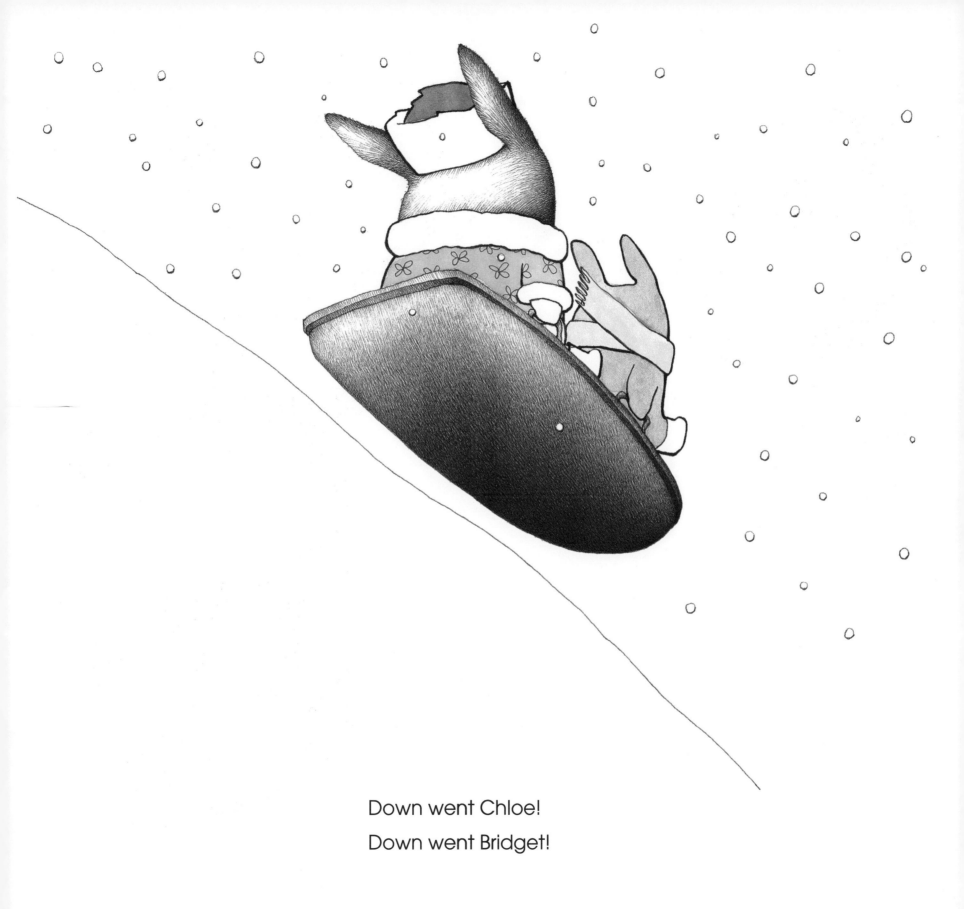

Down went Chloe!

Down went Bridget!

Then everybody went—Pedro too!

"Whoa!" yelled Pedro.

"Watch out!" yelled Sancho.

Over a bump and into the air, Pedro flew!
Thump! Bump! Fump! he went, into the snowbank
at the bottom of the hill.

"How do you like the snow now, Pedro?" asked Sancho.

"I love the snow!"

"Maybe you would like snow in the shape of a ball?"
asked Sancho.

For the rest of the day, Pedro did not feel cold at all.